This snowy activity book belongs to

. . . .

First published in paperback in the United Kingdom by HarperCollins *Children's Books* in 2022

HarperCollins *Children's Books* is a division of HarperCollins*Publishers* Ltd
1 London Bridge Street, London SE1 9GF

www.harpercollins.co.uk

HarperCollins*Publishers*
1st Floor, Watermarque Building, Ringsend Road, Dublin 4, Ireland

1 3 5 7 9 10 8 6 4 2

Text copyright © Nick Butterworth 2022
Illustrations copyright © Nick Butterworth 1989, 1992, 1995, 1996, 1997, 2000, 2001, 2002, 2019, 2022

Black-and-white images redrawn by Mark Burgess copyright © HarperCollins*Publishers* Ltd 1996

Photographs and additional images used under licence from Shutterstock

ISBN: 978-0-00-853596-4

Printed in Poland

MIX
Paper from
responsible sources

FSC
www.fsc.org

FSC™ C007454

This book is produced from independently certified FSC™ paper
to ensure responsible forest management.

For more information visit: www.harpercollins.co.uk/green

One Snowy Night
Activity Book

NICK BUTTERWORTH

HarperCollins *Children's Books*

Staying Safe

Be wise like Percy's friend the owl and follow these top tips when you are out and about in nature:

ALWAYS TAKE AN ADULT WITH YOU.

STAY ON THE PATH OR TRAIL.

DON'T TOUCH, STROKE OR FEED ANY ANIMALS.

KEEP AS QUIET AS POSSIBLE
TO AVOID DISTURBING WILDLIFE.
(AND THEN YOU'LL SEE MORE TOO!)

NEVER DISTURB AN ANIMAL'S HOME.

NEVER EAT ANYTHING YOU FIND ON THE TRAIL.

ALWAYS TAKE YOUR LITTER HOME WITH YOU.

And here are some extra tips for completing the make-and-do activities in this book:

READ THE INSTRUCTIONS CAREFULLY BEFORE STARTING.

ALWAYS ASK AN ADULT TO HELP YOU WITH
ANYTHING SHARP.

"Thank you!"

Welcome to the Park!

Percy works hard looking after the park and the animals who live there, but he still likes to find time for some fun. In the winter, Percy can often be found building a snowman with his friends or curled up with a hot cocoa and a good book.

This book is filled with entertaining activities to enjoy all winter, including Christmas crafts, recipes, games and puzzles, plus over one hundred colourful stickers!

"Have fun!"

Meet Percy's Friends

Percy has lots of animal friends who will be joining in
with the fun activities in this book. Come and say hello!

The hedgehog can usually be
found sleeping in a quiet place.

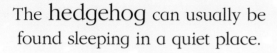

The squirrels know all the
best hiding places in the park!

The fox loves to lend Percy a helping
paw (even if he isn't always that helpful!).

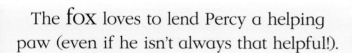

The two ducks do
everything together.

The **owl** spends a lot of her time thinking.

No one knows how many **mice** there are . . .
They never keep still enough to count.

The **rabbits** are so playful and full of energy!

The **badger** will come to the rescue if anyone is in trouble.

The **mole** is a thoughtful and kind chap.

Winter Wonderland

A thick layer of white snow has covered the park.
Percy and the animals cannot wait to play in it!

"Add your stickers of Percy and
his friends playing in the snow."

Snowy Hide-and-seek

Outside in the snow, Percy's friends are playing
a tricky game of hide-and-seek.

"Can you help the mouse find five
of Percy's friends hiding in
the snow?"

"Did you spot
everyone?"

Swirling Snowflakes

It's snowing! Create your very own snowflakes.

YOU WILL NEED:
Paper (21 x 21cm)
Pencil
Safety scissors

"A flurry of snowflakes means winter has arrived."

1. Fold your square in half diagonally to create a triangle.

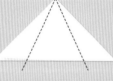

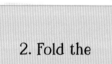

2. Fold the triangle in half again.

3. Fold the points across the triangle along the dotted lines shown in the picture.

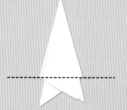

4. Turn it over and trim the top to create a flat line along the top of your triangle.

5. Now draw your pattern on the triangle and cut it out.

6. Unfold your snowflake!

Lost in the Snow

The mice are having great fun on their toboggans, but they seem to have got a bit lost!

"Follow the lines to find out which path the mice need to take to reach Percy."

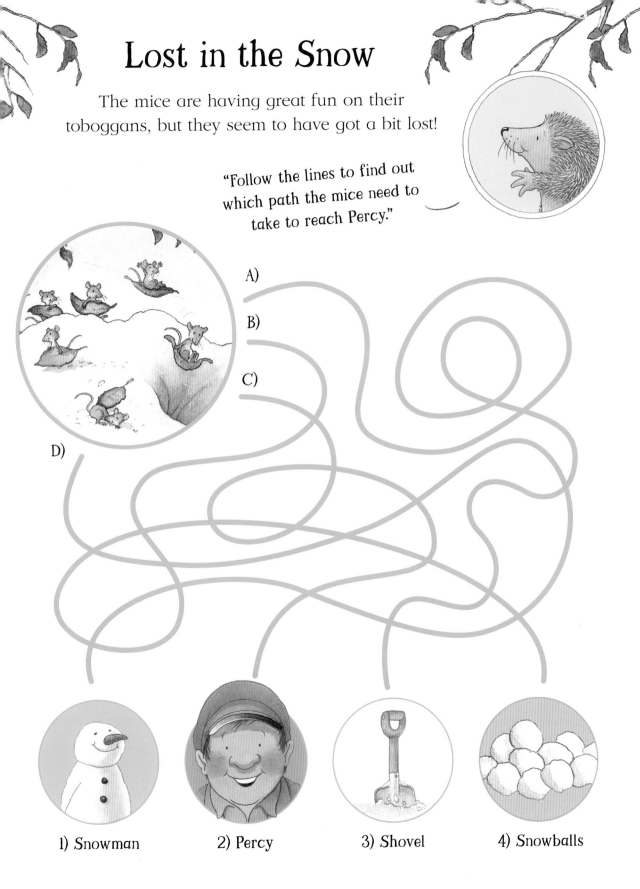

A)

B)

C)

D)

1) Snowman   2) Percy   3) Shovel   4) Snowballs

Countdown to Christmas

The first of December marks the start of the countdown
to Christmas. Let the excitement begin!

"To help you count the days, add a number sticker to these
pages every day in December until you reach Christmas Day."

"I can't wait!"

Marshmallow Snowmen

Make these tasty marshmallow snowmen.

"Add the white chocolate to a bowl and ask an adult to melt it in a microwave, or on the hob. Once it has melted, use the chocolate to stick three marshmallows on top of each other. Place in the fridge for twenty minutes to set.

"Use your icing to create a face and arms for your snowmen! They are now ready to eat!"

YOU WILL NEED:
White chocolate
White marshmallows
Tubes of brown and orange icing
Microwave-safe bowl
Spoon
An adult to help

Cosy Hot Cocoa

When it's chilly outside, a hot cocoa
is sure to warm you up.

YOU WILL NEED:

25g plain chocolate

250ml milk or dairy
alternative

1 tbsp cocoa powder

1 tbsp granulated sugar

Mug

Saucepan

Whisk

An adult to help

"Put all of your
ingredients into a
saucepan. Ask an
adult to heat the pan,
whisking gently, until the
cocoa powder has dissolved and the chocolate
has melted. Pour the mixture into a mug and
wait until it's cool enough to drink.

"If you want an extra special treat, you could add
some whipped cream or pop your marshmallow
snowman (from the previous activity) on top."

Winter Treasures

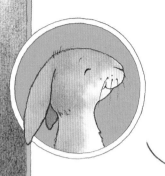

Wrap up warm! Grab your hat and scarf and go out for a walk with your family.

"How many winter treasures can you find? Add a star sticker for each one.

"Draw a picture of your favourite find here."

Something blue . . . . . ⭐

Something cold . . . . . ⭐

Something sparkly . . . ⭐

Something evergreen . . ⭐

Something with berries (don't touch!) . . . . ⭐

Something smooth . . . ⭐

Something tall . . . . . . ⭐

Who's at the Door?

Percy heard a tapping sound.
There was somebody at the door . . .

"Join the dots to reveal who
is at Percy's front door."

Perfect Presents

Make this festive paper to wrap gifts for your friends and family.

YOU WILL NEED:
1 potato
Knife (and an adult to help you!)
Brown paper
Green poster paint
Felt-tip pen

"To create your potato stamp, ask an adult to cut the potato in half. Then draw a Christmas-tree shape on the inside of one half with your felt-tip pen. Ask the adult to carefully cut around the tree shape with the knife. You now have your stamp!

"Dip the stamp into the green paint and press it firmly on to the paper. Cover the paper with lots of terrific trees!"

Deck the Halls

Create these bright and colourful paper chains to decorate your house.

YOU WILL NEED:

Coloured paper strips (approx. 20 x 4cm)

Glue stick

"Take your first paper strip and glue the ends together to create a loop. Thread the next paper strip through the first loop and glue the ends together to create a chain. Keep going until your chain is the perfect length."

Dazzling Decorations

Percy has found the perfect tree.
Now it's time to decorate it.

"Use your holly and
pine-cone stickers to
decorate Percy's tree.
Don't forget to add a
star to the very top!"

"That looks
tree-mendous!"

A Winter's Eve

One cold winter's night, the snow began to fall . . .

"Colour in this picture of Percy
watching the snow drifting down
outside his window."

Gingerbread House

Bake and decorate this amazing
gingerbread house.

YOU WILL NEED:
An adult to help

UTENSILS
Mixing bowl
Wooden spoon
Baking tray
Paper
Pencil
Knife
Safety scissors
Rolling pin

INGREDIENTS
115g unsalted butter
115g light muscovado sugar
1 medium free-range egg
115g golden syrup
375g self-raising flour
2 tsp ground ginger
1 tsp ground cinnamon
1 tube of red icing
1 tube of white icing
Sweets to decorate
(optional)

"Soften the butter and mix with the sugar in a bowl until light and fluffy. Add the egg, golden syrup, flour, ginger and cinnamon. Stir together to form a dough. Knead the dough gently and leave to cool in the fridge for thirty minutes. Ask an adult to preheat the oven to 180°C/160°C fan/gas 4 and grease a baking tray.

"Take your paper and pencil and draw a large rectangle with a triangle on top. Now draw the outline of a person. Cut out both with your safety scissors. These are the templates for your house and gingerbread person.

"After the thirty minutes, roll out the dough on a floured surface and place your templates on top. Ask an adult to carefully cut around the templates. On the house, create a small arch for the door. Repeat until you use all the dough. Place your houses and people on the tray and ask your adult to put them into the oven for twelve to fifteen minutes.

"Once they are cool, you can begin decorating them with the icing. For extra colour, you could add some sweets."

Festive Ornaments

Create these gorgeous decorations to hang on your Christmas tree!

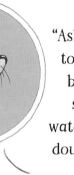

"Ask an adult to preheat the oven to 110°C/90°C fan and grease the baking tray. Mix the flour and salt together. Slowly add the water until the mixture becomes a dough. Knead until it's smooth.

YOU WILL NEED:

250g plain flour

100g table salt

200ml water

Mixing bowl

Baking tray

Spoon

Rolling pin

Knife

Pencil

Poster paints

Paintbrushes

An adult to help

"On a floured surface, roll out the dough and ask an adult to help you cut out Christmas shapes (stars, mittens, trees, hearts etc.). With a pencil, create a hole in each one so you can hang them on the tree.

"Place your decorations on a baking tray and ask your adult to carefully put them in the oven for around three hours. Once they are cool, use your poster paints to decorate."

"Don't be fooled by the dough, these aren't for eating!"

Hard at Work

The snow in the park is beautiful but it's
also a lot of work for Percy as he must clear the paths.

"Can you spot the five
differences between
these pictures?"

Crafty Christmas Trees

Create these fantastic felt Christmas trees
to give to your friends and family.

YOU WILL NEED:
Coloured felt
(including green)
Safety scissors
Glue stick

"Take your green felt and carefully cut
out a Christmas-tree shape. Now take
your coloured felt and cut out lots of
circles and stars. Once you've done this,
arrange them on your tree and glue them
in place. Don't forget to put a special
star at the top of the tree."

"That looks great!"

Twinkle, Twinkle

On a frosty winter's night, you can see lots of stars shining in the sky.

"To make your own sparkling star, place your first ice-lolly stick vertically and glue a second diagonally across it. Then take a third ice-lolly stick and glue that diagonally going the other way to create a star. Once the glue dries, you can decorate your star with buttons. Choose a big button for the centre."

YOU WILL NEED:
3 ice-lolly sticks
Assorted blue buttons
Glue stick

"What a superstar!"

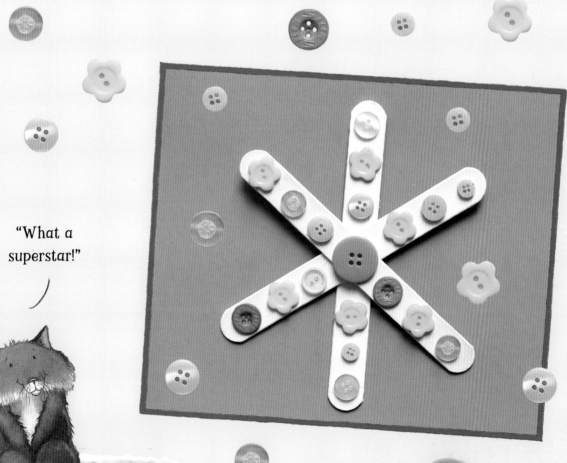

Winter Birdwatch

Many birds from cold countries fly to warmer places for the winter. This means there may be new birds to see in your garden.

"To start birdwatching, either pop outside with a trusted adult or sit by a window. Make sure you look everywhere – up in the sky, in the trees and on the ground. Remember to be quiet and still so you don't scare off the birds.

"Draw pictures of the birds you spot here."

Winter Walks

A crisp, sunny winter's day is a
great time to see nature.

"Ask a trusted adult to take you out for a
walk in the local park or countryside.

Tick the items as
you find them.

- ( ) Pine cones
- ( ) Icicles
- ( ) Robins
- ( ) Pawprints
- ( ) Evergreen trees
- ( ) Holly (don't touch!)

"Draw pictures of the
things you spot here."

Jolly Reindeer

Make these marvellous reindeer decorations to hang on your tree.

YOU WILL NEED:
Pine cone
2 googly eyes
Pom-pom
Brown pipe cleaners
String
Glue stick

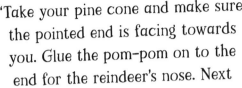

"Take your pine cone and make sure the pointed end is facing towards you. Glue the pom-pom on to the end for the reindeer's nose. Next add two googly eyes. Cut your pipe cleaner into 7cm lengths. Twist one pipe cleaner around another, towards the top, to create your first antler. Repeat to create the second. Glue these to the top of your reindeer's head. Wrap the string round the middle of the pine cone and knot, then tie the two ends together to create a loop.

"Now your reindeer is ready for the tree!"

Christmas Wreath

Create your own fabulously festive wreath.

YOU WILL NEED:

Green felt

Red felt

Red ribbon

Decorations
(such as pom-poms,
sequins or stars)

Safety scissors

Glue stick

Plate (17cm diameter)

Drinking glass
(9cm diameter)

Pen

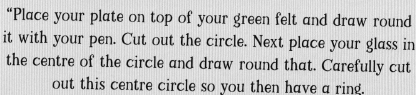

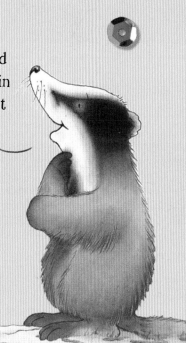

"Place your plate on top of your green felt and draw round it with your pen. Cut out the circle. Next place your glass in the centre of the circle and draw round that. Carefully cut out this centre circle so you then have a ring.

"Take your red ribbon and tie a small bow. Glue that to the wreath. Now decorate with your pom-poms, sequins and stars."

Sleep Tight

In the winter some animals curl up in a safe place and go to sleep until the cold weather ends. This is called hibernation.

"Unscramble the names of these animals who hibernate."

1) BLEEUMBBE
....

2) TOISEROT
....

3) GOHEDGEH
....

4) REAB
....

Ice Art

Become one of the coolest artists and
make your own ice paintings.

YOU WILL NEED:
Water
Food colouring
Ice-lolly sticks
Ice-cube tray
Paper

"Pour water into the ice-cube
tray, but make sure it isn't too full.
Add a drop of food colouring to
each of the compartments and
mix well. Add an ice-lolly stick to each compartment,
and carefully place the tray in the freezer. The
ice paints will need around twelve hours to freeze
properly. You can then remove them from the tray.

"You are now ready
to paint! Cover your
working surface with
a wipeable cover or
newspaper, as food
colouring can stain.
Hold the wooden
sticks and begin
painting on your
paper."

"That looks
n-ice!"

Merry Christmas!

Wish your friends and family a merry Christmas with these superb cards.

YOU WILL NEED:
A4 card
Triangle of card
(10 x 10 x 8cm)
String
Safety scissors
Glue stick
Sequins
Pom-poms

"Fold your A4 card in half to create the base for your card. Next take your triangle of card and glue the string to the top point. Wrap the string all the way down the triangle, until it is completely covered as if with a strand of twinkly lights. Cut the string and glue the loose end to the back of the triangle. You now have your Christmas tree.

"Glue the tree to the card, and then you can decorate it with sequins and pom-poms for its baubles. The card is now ready for you to add a special message inside."

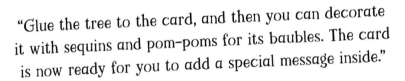

Gorgeous Gifts

Make sure your gifts look fantastically festive with these creative gift tags.

YOU WILL NEED:
Kraft-paper gift tags
Glue stick
Red-and-white string
Buttons
Black pen

Snowman Gift Tag

"Glue a large white button for the snowman's tummy and a smaller one for his head on to a Kraft-paper tag. Create a bow with your string and glue it on for the scarf. You can use your black pen to give him a little hat.

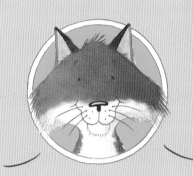

Baubles Gift Tag

"Glue three coloured buttons to the tag. With your black pen, draw lines from the top of the tag to the buttons and add little bows above them.

"Take a length of string and fold it in half, pushing the loop through the hole in the gift tag. Thread the ends through the loop and pull. Your gift tags are now ready to add to your presents."

A Tight Squeeze

It was great fun when all the animals
came to stay with Percy, but there
wasn't much room left in the bed!

"Use your crayons to colour in this
picture of Percy and all his friends."

A Snowy Sleepover

One snowy night all the animals arrived
at Percy's hut in search of a warm bed.

"Everyone has found a bed for the night,
but they've made quite a mess. Look carefully –
can you spot the hidden objects?"

Key

Scissors

Vase

Toothbrush

Golf balls

Thimble

Snowy Footprints

A perfect blanket of snow lies undisturbed
in the park. But, wait, what's that?

"Follow the lines to find out who
the footprints belong to."

1)

2)

3)

4)

A) Squirrel

B) Bird

C) Fox

D) Badger

Winter Berries

During the winter, many birds and animals
eat the berries and nuts from the trees.

*"Using your crayons, colour in the trees
and bushes and draw lots of bright,
juicy berries for the birds and animals."*

*"Never eat any berries you find
outside – they can often be
poisonous for humans."*

Dear Father Christmas

Every year Percy writes a special
letter to Father Christmas.

"Practise writing your letter to
Father Christmas here. You can decorate
the letter with your star stickers."

DEAR FATHER CHRISTMAS,

· ·

· ·

· ·

· ·

· ·

· ·

· ·

FROM,

· ·

· ·

Stocking Presents

Percy and the animals hang their
stockings by the fire on Christmas Eve.

"Use your crayons to colour in
the stocking. Draw a special present
poking out for Percy."

"Ooh! How
exciting."

Snow Days

Clearing the snow is hot work,
even in the cold weather.

"Use your square stickers to finish the
picture of Percy."

"I like to keep warm by
going underground."

Festive Fun

Christmas is a great time to have a party,
and no party is complete without games!

"Here are some of
my favourite festive
games to play!"

What's in the Stocking?

Take a Christmas stocking and fill it
with objects from around your home.
Tie it up with ribbon to stop anyone
peeking. Now pass it around the
players and have everyone write down
what they think is in the stocking. The
person with the most correct guesses wins.

Pin the Carrot on the Snowman

Take an A3 piece of paper and draw a
snowman's head without a nose. On another
piece of paper, draw a carrot nose for every
player. Cut these out and attach double-sided
tape to their backs. Taking it in turns,
each player is blindfolded and must
attempt to place their carrot where
the snowman's nose should be.
The closest attempt wins.

Sleeping Reindeer

Choose someone to be Father Christmas.
All other players are reindeer and must
lie on the floor very still with their eyes
closed. Then Father Christmas must
try to get the reindeer to move without
touching them. If a reindeer
moves, they are out. The last
player left "sleeping" wins.

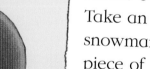

Sparkling Snowglobe

Make your very own magical snowglobe.

"Decorate the edges of your pine cone with the silver paint. When it's dry, glue the pine cone to the inside of the jam-jar lid. Next ask an adult to help add the glycerine to the jar and top up with water, making sure to leave room at the top. Add the glitter and stir.

"Line the neck of the jar with glue. Turn the pine cone upside down, pop it into the water and screw on the lid. Wait for the glue to dry and turn the jar carefully to test for leaks. Finish your snowglobe by adding a festive ribbon!"

All Wrapped Up

The fox dislikes being cold, so he
borrows cosy clothes from Percy.

"The fox looks very
warm! Can you spot the
five differences between
these images?"

Stained-glass Biscuits

Bake these colourful festive biscuits
for your friends and family.

YOU WILL NEED:
An adult to help

UTENSILS
Baking tray
Parchment paper
Mixing bowl
Electric whisk
Rolling pin
Knife
Chopstick
Ribbon

INGREDIENTS
100g unsalted butter
75g muscovado sugar
1 medium free-range egg
200g plain flour
$\frac{1}{2}$ tsp baking powder
1 tsp nutmeg
1 tsp ground cinnamon
1 tsp vanilla extract
Boiled sweets

"Ask an adult to preheat the oven to 180°C/160°C fan/gas 4 and line a baking tray with parchment paper.

"In your mixing bowl, whisk the butter and sugar together until light and fluffy. Add the egg and mix thoroughly. Stir in the flour, baking powder, nutmeg, cinnamon and vanilla extract. Keep mixing until it forms a dough.

"Put the dough on to a floured surface and roll out. Cut out your biscuits in your favourite Christmas shapes and pop them on to the baking tray. Ask an adult to carefully cut out the centre of the biscuits with a knife. Place a boiled sweet in the middle of each biscuit.

"Ask an adult to carefully place the tray in the oven and cook for fifteen minutes. While the biscuits are still warm, have your adult put a hole in the top of each one with the chopstick. Wait for the biscuits to cool, thread ribbons through the holes, and then they are ready to hang on the tree."

Little Robin Redbreast

Robins can often be seen in the garden in the winter.

"Join the dashes to make the robin appear.
Then colour it in with your crayons. Don't
forget its bright-red tummy!"

A Field of Snowmen

When the snow falls, Percy and the animals love to build snowmen.

"Using your crayons, decorate these snowmen. You can use your stickers to add scarves and gloves too."

"What do you call a snowman party?

A snowball."

Frozen Bubbles

Watch the ice crystals form in these spectacular frozen bubbles.

YOU WILL NEED:
32g granulated sugar
425ml warm water
60ml washing-up liquid
Mixing bowl
Spoon
Reusable straw
A very cold day
(0°C or lower)
An adult to help

"To make your bubble mixture, add the sugar to your bowl and pour over the warm water. Stir until the sugar dissolves. Then add the washing-up liquid and pop into the fridge to chill for at least thirty minutes.

"Take your mixture outside and dip your straw in. Next gently blow on the end of the straw (don't suck!) to create a bubble and place it gently on to a cold surface. Try to find somewhere sheltered from the wind, otherwise your bubble may pop.

"Once your bubble is in place, you can watch the magical ice crystals start to appear!

"Remember to wrap up warm when you are outside in cold temperatures and take a trusted adult with you."

Winter Wonders

From snow and icicles to evergreen trees, there are so many amazing things to love about winter.

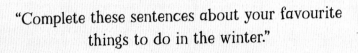
"Complete these sentences about your favourite things to do in the winter."

My favourite thing about winter is ....

....

My favourite warm food is ....

....

My favourite outdoor winter activity is ....

....

My favourite indoor winter activity is ....

....

I like to keep warm by ....

....

The best place I went this winter was ....

....

It's Snow-time!

Lights, camera, action! Christmas is the perfect time to put on a show for your loved ones.

"Complete these sentences to come up with the story for your play."

The main character is . . . .

Their best friend is . . . .

They live in . . . .

They decide to . . . .

. . . .

At the end they . . . .

"Could we be in your story?"

. . . .

"To create the characters for your story, take your coloured card and cut out the shape of each character with your safety scissors. Then glue them to ice-lolly sticks and decorate with festive pom-poms. You can use the ice-lolly stick to move your characters around. Your characters are now ready to take centre stage!"

Playful Penguins

These cute penguins make the
perfect Christmas gift.

YOU WILL NEED:
Cardboard tube
Black poster paint
White, black, yellow,
red and pink paper
Googly eyes
Safety scissors
Glue stick

"Paint your cardboard tube black and leave to dry.
Cut out two flippers and spiky-head feathers from your
black paper. Take your white paper and cut out a large
circle. With the yellow paper, cut out two long, spiky
eyebrows. Take the red paper, cut a triangle and fold
it down the middle to create a crease. Next cut
out two feet from the pink paper.

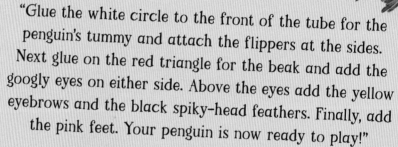

"Glue the white circle to the front of the tube for the
penguin's tummy and attach the flippers at the sides.
Next glue on the red triangle for the beak and add the
googly eyes on either side. Above the eyes add the yellow
eyebrows and the black spiky-head feathers. Finally, add
the pink feet. Your penguin is now ready to play!"

Frosty Friend

Make this fantastic
chilled-out polar bear.

YOU WILL NEED:
White cardboard
Black pen
Glue stick
Safety scissors

"Take your white card and cut out one large
circle for the bear's body and a slightly
smaller one for the head. Now cut out one
circle for the muzzle, four small circles for the
paws and two semi-circles for the ears."

"Glue the ears and the muzzle to the head and attach to
the body. Now add the four paws. Use your black pen to
draw the face and other details for your polar bear."

Terrific Toboggans

When it snows in the park, you'll see the mice and squirrels having lots of fun on their toboggans. Everyone loves tobogganing!

"Use your stickers to add the mice on their leaf-toboggans to this picture.

"How many squirrels can you spot?"

"Wheee!"

Falling Snowflakes

The magical thing about snowflakes
is that each one is different and unique.

"Use your stickers to cover this
page with drifting snowflakes."

Brilliant Bunting

Deck the halls with this superb zesty bunting.

"Take your orange peel and cut it into your favourite Christmas shapes (stars, trees, hearts, etc.) using your safety scissors. Ask an adult to carefully put a hole in the top of each with a darning needle. Pop them on a plate and leave them to dry in a warm, sunny place for two to three days.

"Once the pieces are dry, you can thread them on to your string to create festive bunting to decorate your house!"

Safe and Snug!

On a snowy night, there's nothing nicer than snuggling up in bed.

"Use your crayons to colour in this picture of Percy and the squirrel.

"Sleep tight!"

A Letter to Percy

There was a mysterious letter in Percy's letterbox this morning.

"Use the code to work out what the letter says and who it is from!"

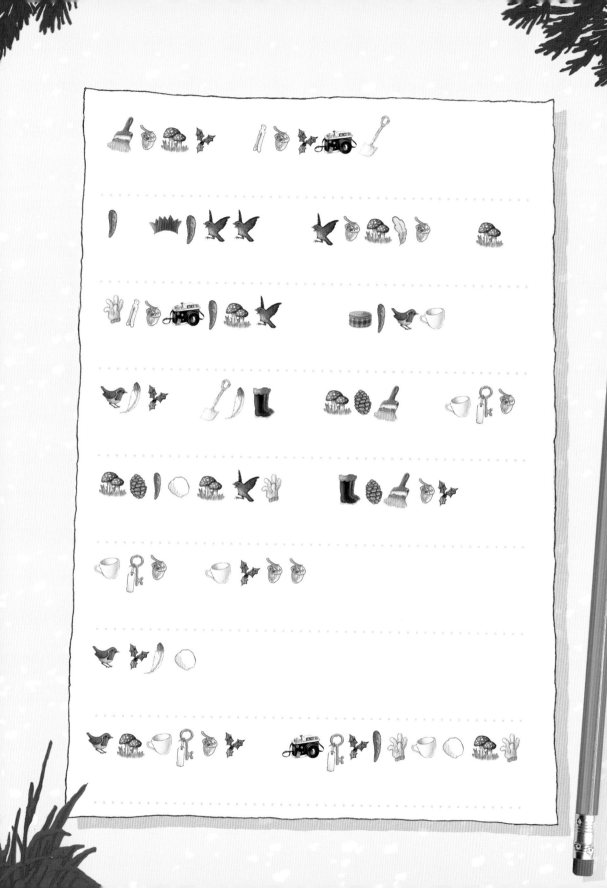

Lost Property

While Percy was shovelling snow, he put his hat, gloves and scarf down – but now they are missing!

"Follow the lines to find out what objects each animal borrowed."

A) Squirrel B) Owl C) Mice D) Badger

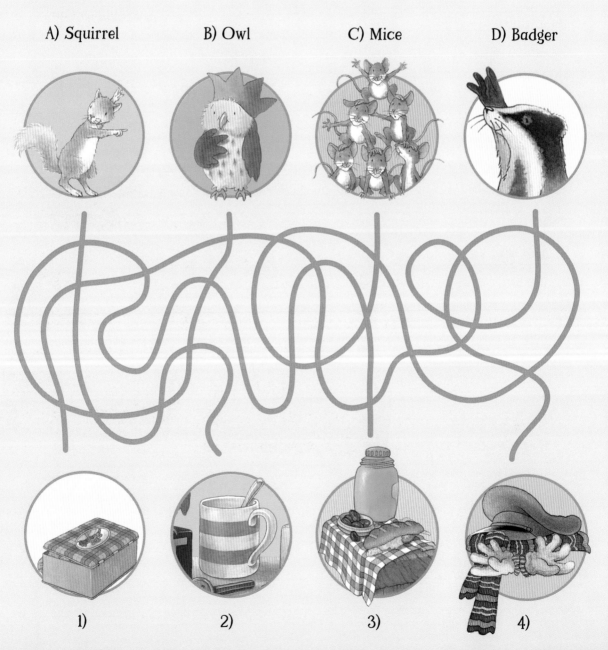

1)   2)   3)   4)

Spring Is Coming!

Winter is the perfect time to plant bulbs ready for the spring.

"With help from an adult, use your trowel to prepare a hole in the soil for each of your bulbs. Pop the bulbs carefully into the holes with their pointed ends facing upwards. Now cover over with soil and water. Then make sure to wash your hands.

"To choose the best time to plant your bulbs, always follow the instructions on the packet.

YOU WILL NEED:

Bulbs
(such as daffodils, snowdrops, tulips)

Trowel

Garden border or pot with peat-free compost

Watering can

An adult to help

"Now wait for those first little green shoots to appear – then you know spring is on the way!"

Answers

Snowy Hide-and-seek

Lost in the Snow
Path 'C' leads to Percy.

Who's at the Door?
The rabbits are at Percy's door.

Hard at Work

Sleep Tight
1) Bumblebee 2) Tortoise
3) Hedgehog 4) Bear

A Snowy Sleepover

Snowy Footprints
1) D, 2) B, 3) A, 4) C

All Wrapped Up

Terrific Toboggans
There are three squirrels in the picture.

A Letter to Percy
Dear Percy, I will leave a special gift
for you and the animals under the
tree. From, Father Christmas

Lost Property
A) 2, B) 3, C) 4, D) 1